What shall I draw?

Contents

Draw a pig

1

2

3

4

5

6

7

8

Lying down pig

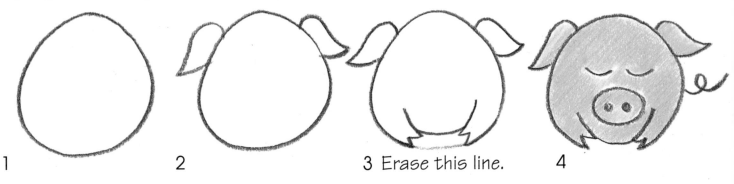

1

2

3 Erase this line.

4

Sideways pig

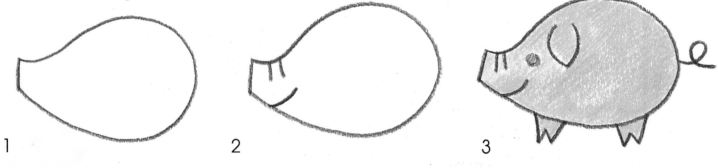

1

2

3

2

A piggy scene

You could draw any kind of flowers. These are tulips.

For lettuce leaves, draw wiggly green shapes.

Green spikes for grass

Wavy brown lines for mud

Now how about... a pig family at dinner time?

Draw a sea monster

1

2

3

4

A sea monster battle

Soft blue crayoning for the sky.

Drops of water.

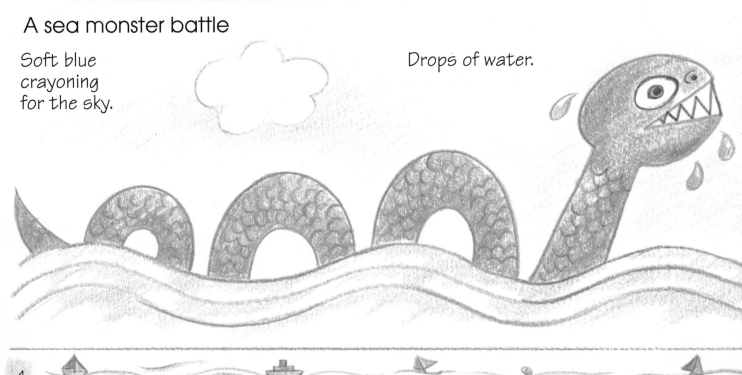

5

6

Draw a pattern on his body.

7

Draw a cloud.

Draw sharp teeth.

Draw a snail

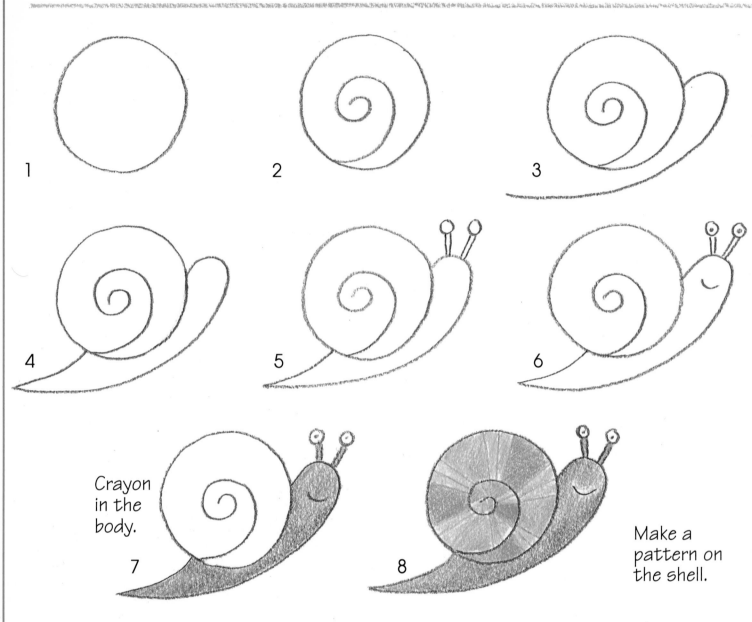

1

2

3

4

5

6

Crayon in the body.

7

8

Make a pattern on the shell.

Draw the children

Draw some little baby snails.

Make the shells different.

Make a picture story

1

2

3

Draw snails on a flower.

Add some grass and leaves.

Open mouth

Jagged bite in the leaf

4

5

6

Now how about... A snail race?

Draw a space rocket

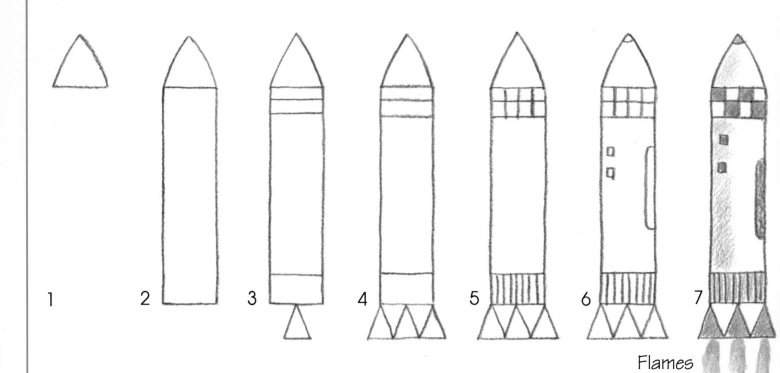

1   2   3   4   5   6   7

Flames

A rocket launch

1 Draw a tall ladder for the launch tower.

2 Add zig zag lines.

3

Dots for sparks

Add clouds of grey smoke.

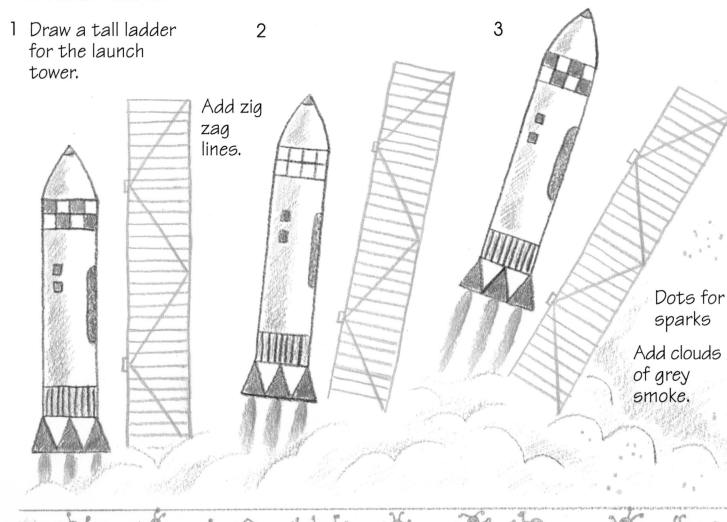

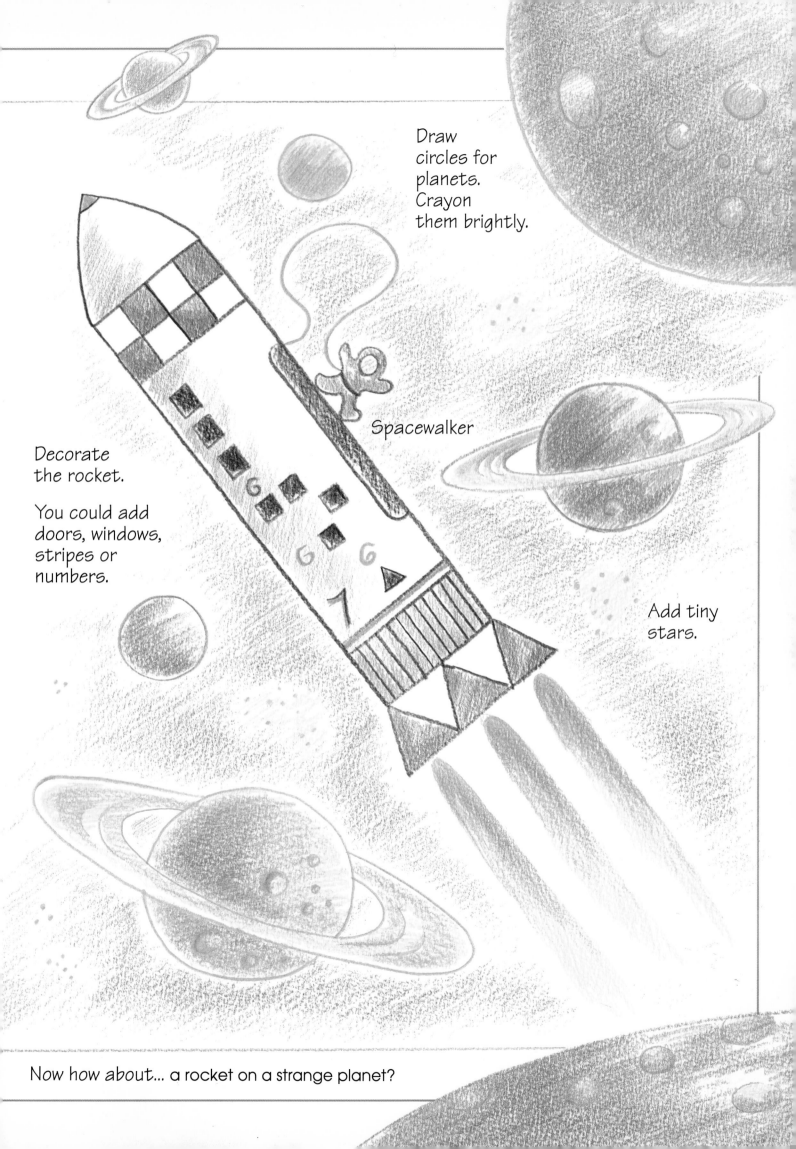

Draw circles for planets. Crayon them brightly.

Spacewalker

Decorate the rocket.

You could add doors, windows, stripes or numbers.

Add tiny stars.

Now how about... a rocket on a strange planet?

Draw an owl

Start with a branch.

Draw a dot here.

Draw scribbly stripes on the wings.

Shade around the eyes.

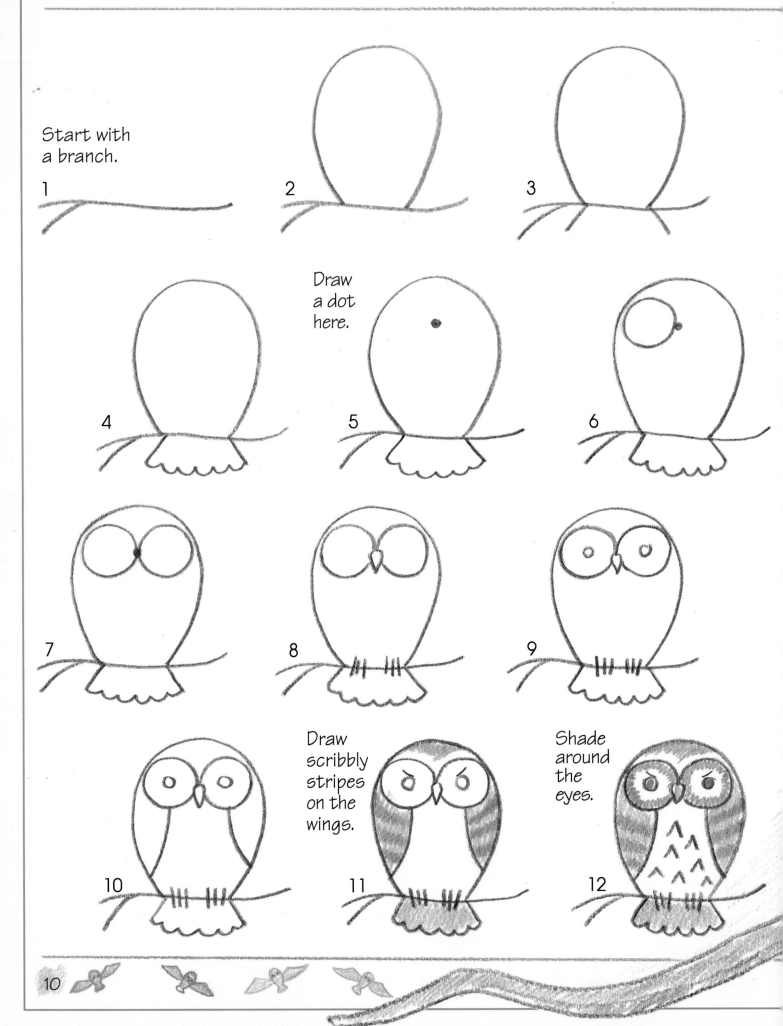

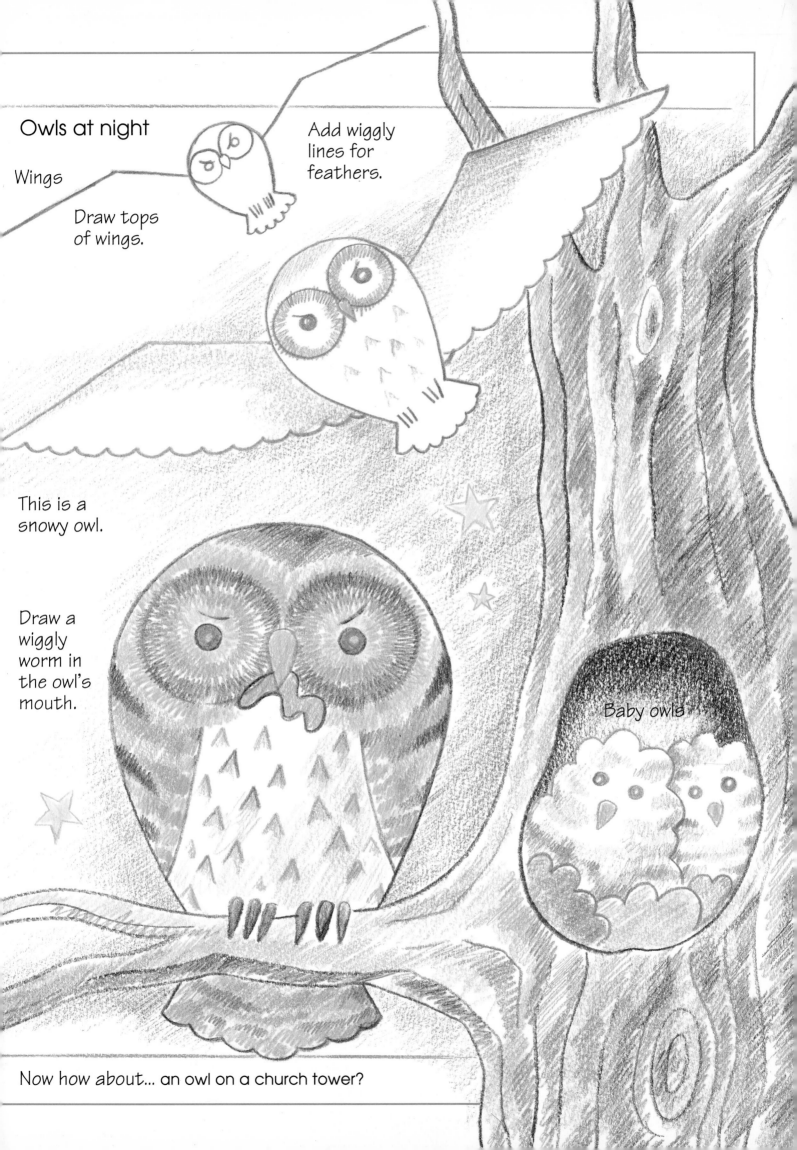

Owls at night

Wings

Draw tops of wings.

Add wiggly lines for feathers.

This is a snowy owl.

Draw a wiggly worm in the owl's mouth.

Baby owls

Now how about... an owl on a church tower?

Draw a submarine

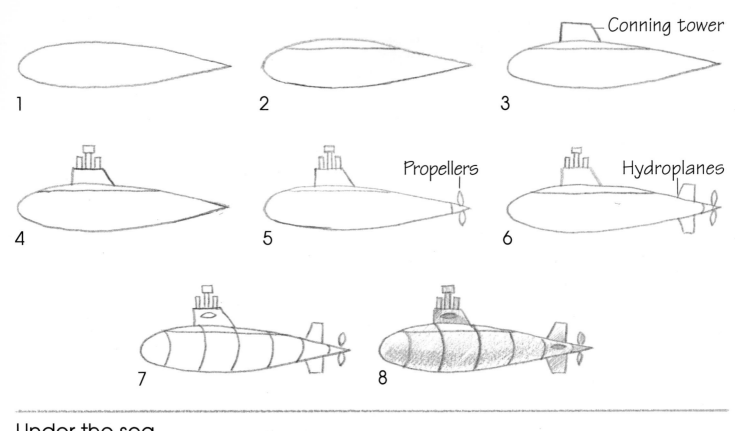

Conning tower

1

2

3

Propellers

4

5

Hydroplanes

6

7

8

Under the sea

Draw a battle with a giant
octopus. Add sea creatures,
shells and seaweed.

In the sea

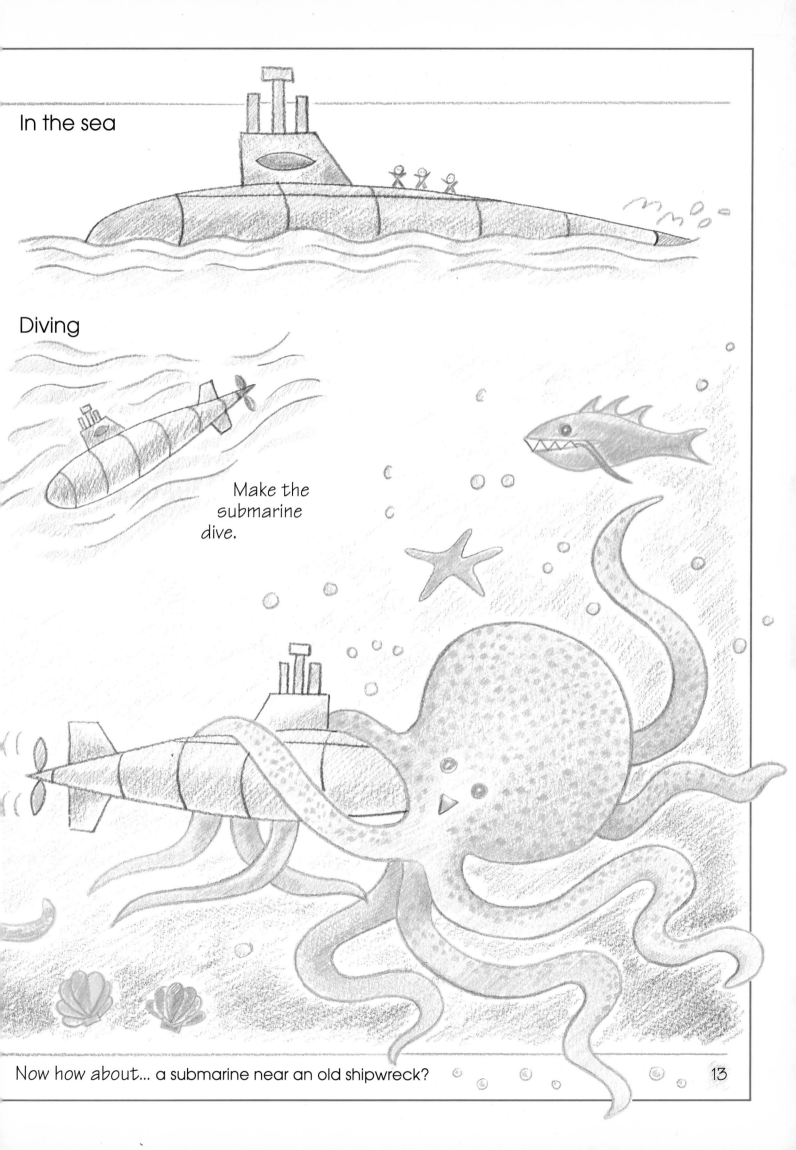

Diving

Make the
submarine
dive.

Now how about... a submarine near an old shipwreck?

13

Draw a tiger

1

2

3

4

5

6

7

8

9

10 Erase the lines you don't need.

11 Crayon the body, but leave some white patches.

12 Add scribbly stripes.

Sleeping tiger

Leaping tiger

Draw a tree for the tiger to lie on.

Now how about... some tigers prowling in the grass?

15

Draw a wizard

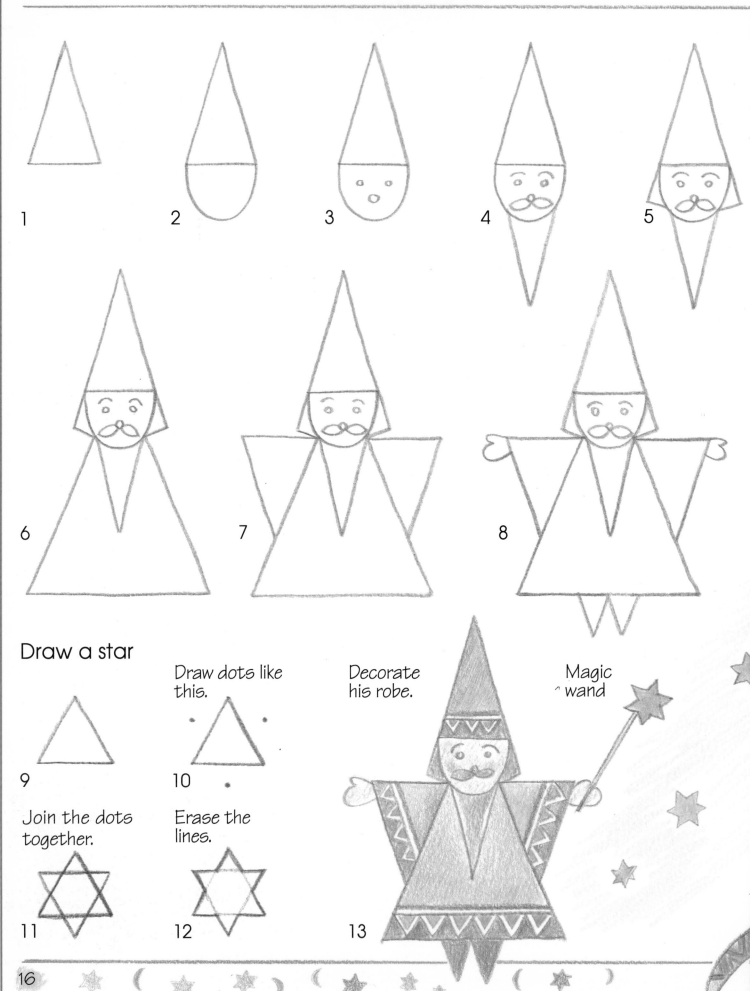

1

2

3

4

5

6

7

8

Draw a star

Draw dots like this.

Decorate his robe.

Magic wand

9

10

Join the dots together.

Erase the lines.

11

12

13

16

Draw some stars to show he is casting a spell.

Spell book

Snake

Cauldron

Draw a helicopter

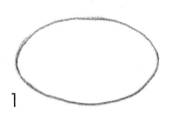

1

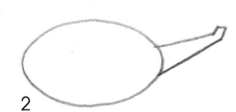

2

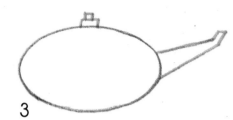

3

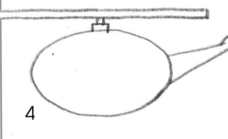

4

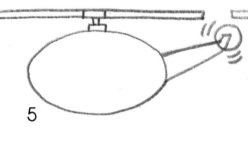

5

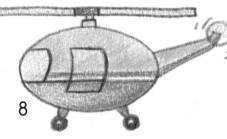

6

Lines around the tail propeller make it seem to move.

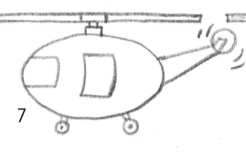

7

8

Crayon your helicopter.

More flying 'copters

These helicopters are rescuing people.

This one has skids underneath, so it can land on the water.

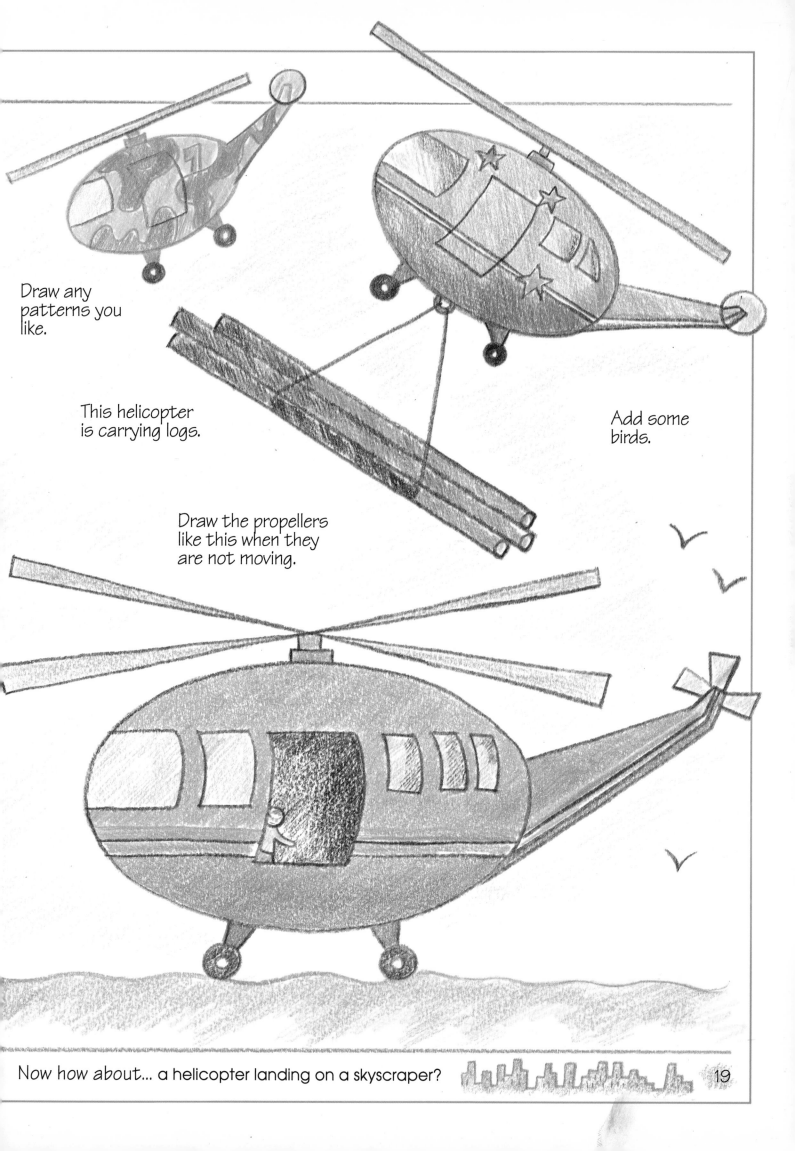

Draw any patterns you like.

This helicopter is carrying logs.

Draw the propellers like this when they are not moving.

Add some birds.

Now how about... a helicopter landing on a skyscraper?

19

Draw a cat

Snoozing cat

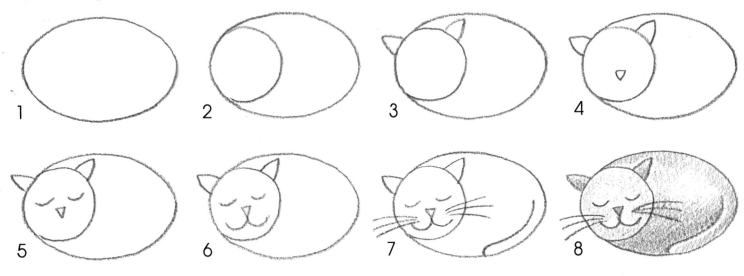

1 2 3 4

5 6 7 8

Standing cat

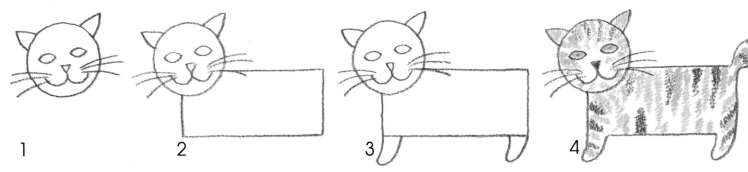

1 2 3 4

Crouching cat

1

Draw the body
in pencil first.

2

Erase one end.
Draw in the head.

Lapping cat

Add a
tongue and
a saucer of
milk.

3

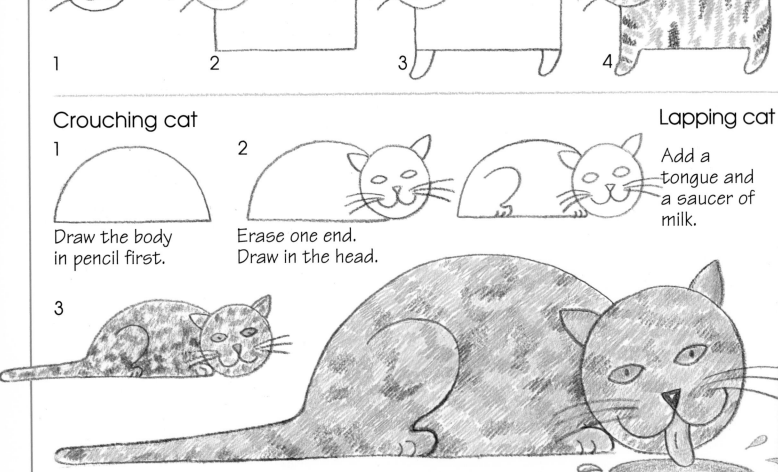

Sitting cat

1

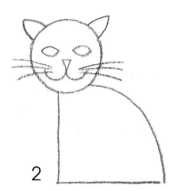
2

3

4

Cat family

Draw a large sitting cat for the mother.

Comfy cat

Draw the snoozing cat on a cushion.

Don't forget their tails.

Now draw the kittens. Add two paws beneath each head.

Draw a box for the kittens.

Now how about... a cat on a roof...a cat chasing a mouse?

Draw circles

Try drawing circles. If it's too hard, you could draw around a cup.

Dinner

Fish

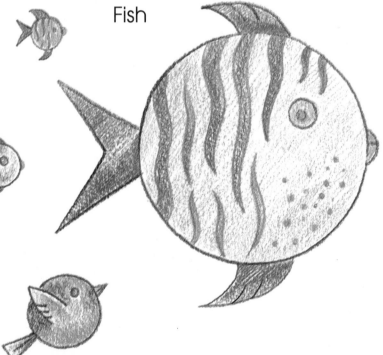

Snowman

Robin

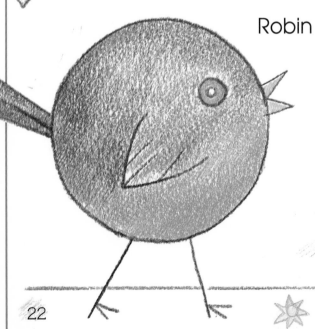

Apple

Clock

Balloon

Mouse

Lion

Now how about... a spider?... what else can you think of?

23

Draw a clown

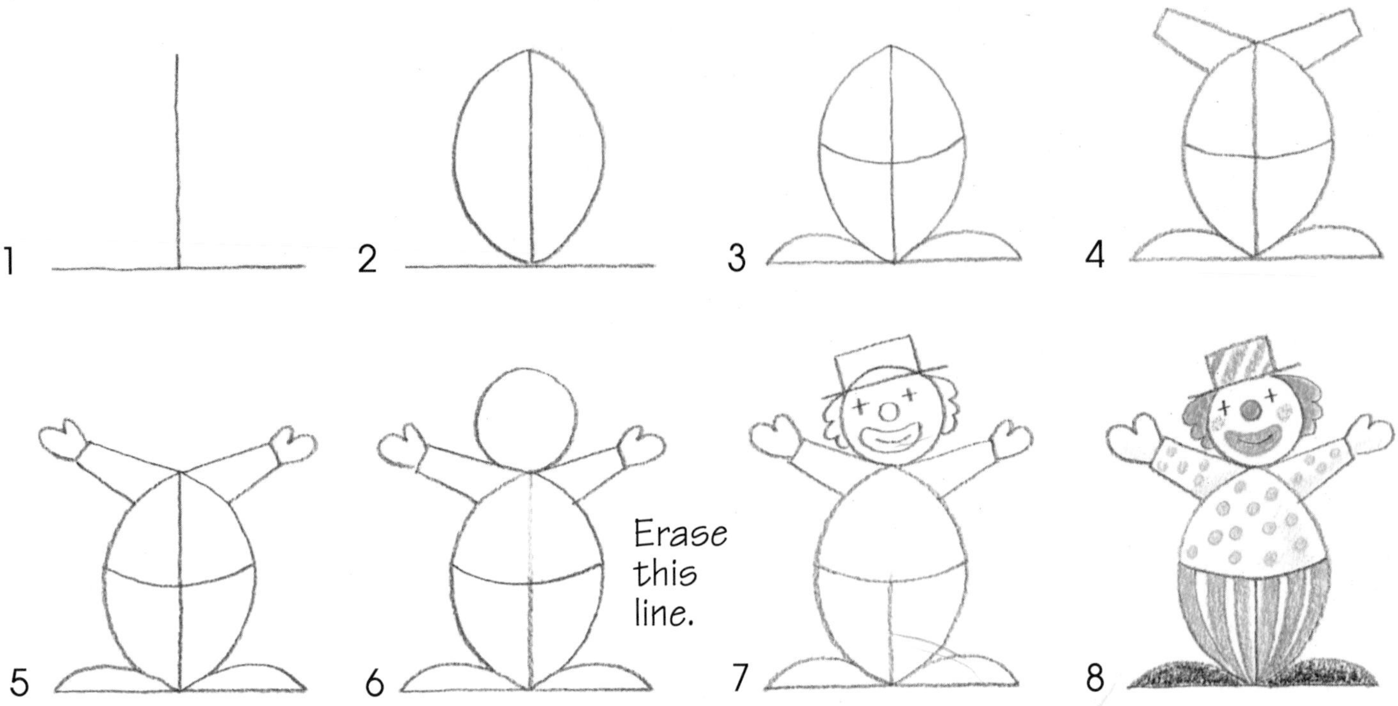

1

2

3

4

5

6 Erase this line.

7

8

Clowning around

You could draw the arms in different positions.

Decorate the clown however you like.

Add some balls for a juggling clown.

Draw a ballerina

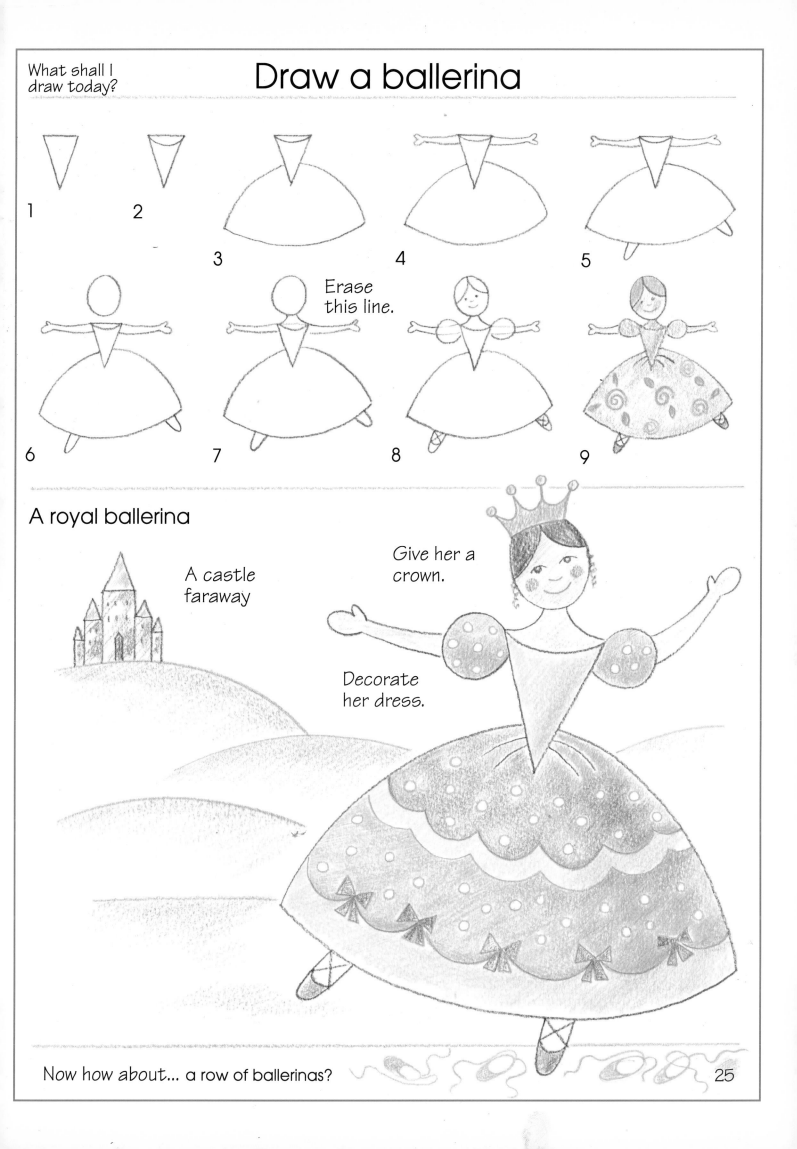

1

2

3

4

5

6

7
Erase this line.

8

9

A royal ballerina

A castle faraway

Give her a crown.

Decorate her dress.

Draw a teddy

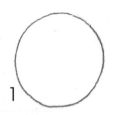

1

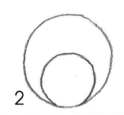

2

3

4

5

6

7

8

9

Walking Teddy

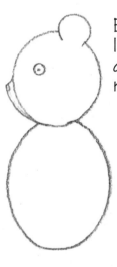

Erase the lines you don't need.

Sitting teddy

Erase the lines you don't need.

Shouting teddy

Draw the mouth open.

Teddy bears' picnic

Teddies playing

Shading for straight fur.

Squiggles for curly fur.

Now how about... teddy bears at a swimming pool?

Draw a castle

Leave gaps here.

1

2

3

4

5

6

7

8

9

Flags

Windows

10

Draw lines going across.

11

Add lines going down.

Crayon your
castle.

A castle on fire

Red and
orange flames.

Add clouds
of smoke.

Make all the flames
go the same way.

Wiggly blue lines
for the castle moat.

Buckets of water.

Now how about... a castle in a storm with lightning?

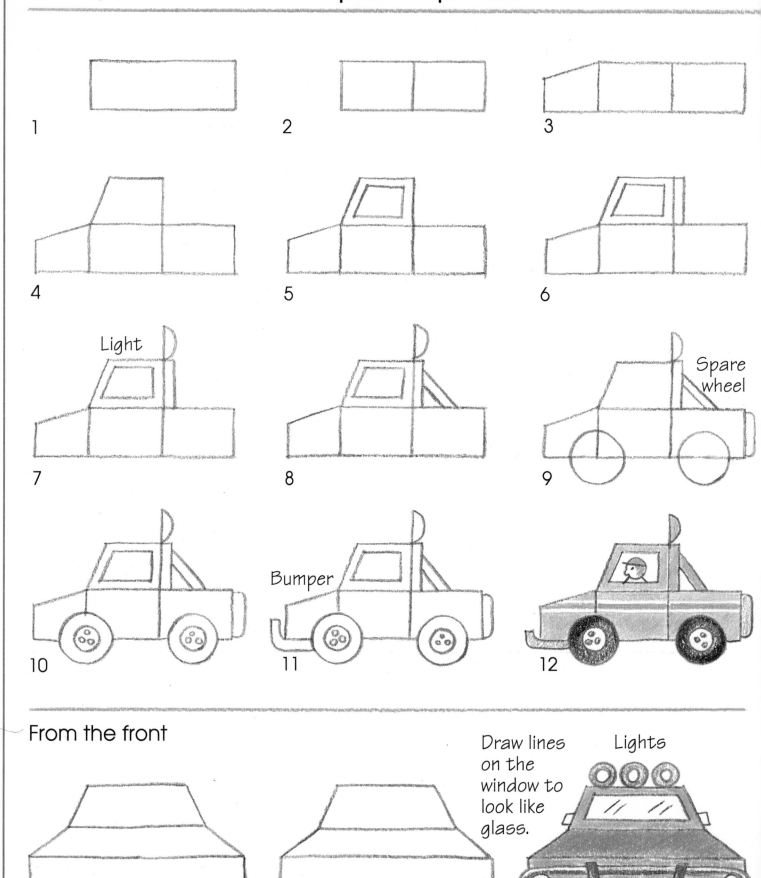

Draw a pick-up truck

1

2

3

4

5

6

Light

7

8

Spare wheel

9

10

Bumper

11

12

From the front

1

2

Draw lines on the window to look like glass.

Lights

3

Draw a car

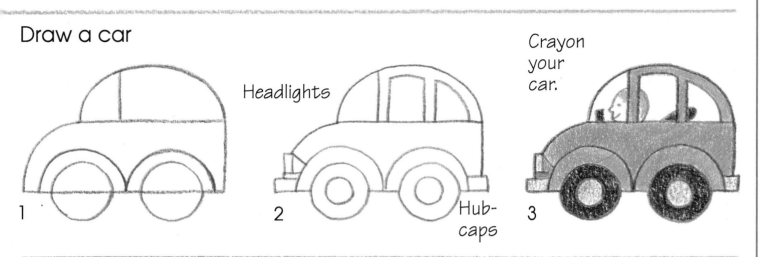

Headlights

1

2

Hub-
caps

Crayon
your
car.

3

Pick-up trucks at work

Draw a pick-up
truck pulling a car
out of a lake.

Add scenery.

Pick-up trucks can go
up steep slopes.

Now how about... a pick-up truck rescuing a racing car?

Things to do with your drawings

Mounting

1

Take a piece of paper or cardboard, a little bigger than your drawing.

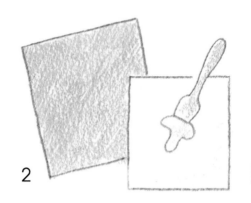

2

Spread glue thinly over the back of the drawing. Put it in the middle of the mount.

3

With clean hands, smooth your drawing down firmly.

Fancy mounts

Cut a wiggly edge for your mount with scissors.

Draw a simple pattern on your mount.

Decorate your mount with wrapping paper.

Sprinkle glitter on your mount or stick on shiny stars.

Making a shaped card

Fold a piece of cardboard in half. Glue your drawing close to the fold. Leaving the folded side, cut around your drawing, close to the edge.

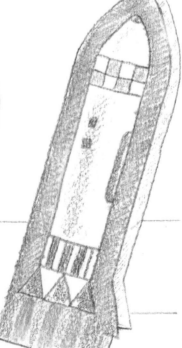

What shall I paint?

Contents

Paint a parrot

1. Paint the body, like this.

2. Make a hand print on either side for the wings.

3. Paint the tail. Add wingtips.

4. Paint the head.

5. Add a beak, eye and claws.

6. Add tips to the wings and tail.

To paint a perching parrot, make a hand print on a slant.

Then paint the rest of the parrot as before.

Now how about...a row of perching parrots on a long branch?

To print a leafy
background, paint
the rough side of a
leaf and press it
onto the paper.

Paint a cat on a rug

1. Draw a cat's head in crayon near one side of your sheet of paper.

2. Now draw its body. Add a face, tail and whiskers. Go over the lines again.

3. With a new crayon, draw a big oblong around the cat. Add stripes and patterns.

4. Now paint over the cat, using runny black paint. The cat will show through.

5. Paint the rug area in different shades. The patterns will show through.

6. Crayon a fringe at both ends of your rug to finish off the picture.

You could use only one shade of paint for the rug.

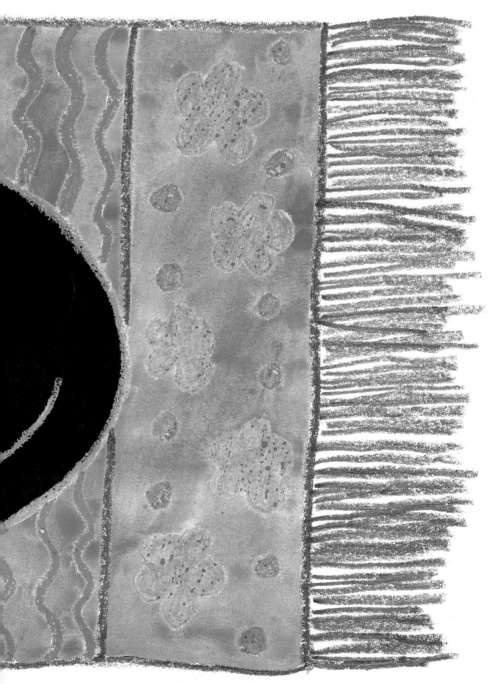

A cat in the grass

Draw a cat with a yellow crayon. Crayon flowers around it. Paint over the cat with orange paint and over the flowers with green paint.

 Now how about... a window with patterned curtains?

Paint a monster

1. Fold your paper in
half. Press down firmly
and then open it.

2. With a damp cloth,
wipe on some blue
paint for the sky.

3. Paint a tree shape
down one side. Fold
your paper again and
press down firmly.

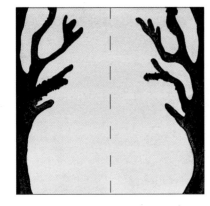

4. When you open it
there will be trees
down both edges of
the paper. Allow to dry.

5. Paint some blobs
near the middle of the
paper like this. Use
monster-ish shades.

6. Fold and press the
paper again. Open it
out. When the paint is
dry, add eyes and teeth.

Now how about... an alien?

Paint a scary picture

Haunted woods

 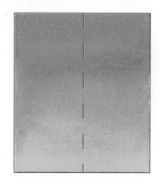  

1. Fold your paper in half. Press down firmly, then open it out again.

2. With a damp cloth, wipe on some red and yellow paint.

3. Paint trees on one side with runny black paint. Fold and press.

4. When dry, paint scary eyes among your spooky trees.

A dragon

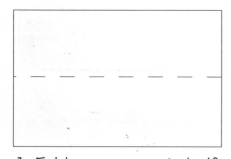  

1. Fold your paper in half, press down firmly and open it out again.

2. Paint some blobs near the middle. Fold and press, then open the paper.

3. Paint the head, legs and tail when dry.

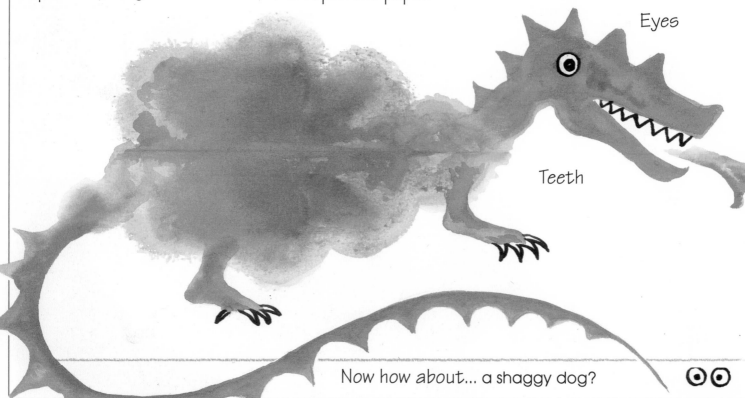

Eyes

Teeth

Now how about... a shaggy dog?

Paint penguins on the ice

Ice

Sea

Icy sea

1. With a damp cloth, wipe white paint over one end of the paper.

2. In the same way, wipe blue paint over the rest of it.

3. Paint some clingwrap white. Press the painted side over the blue.

4. Lift it off gently and repeat until all the blue is patterned with white.

Penguins

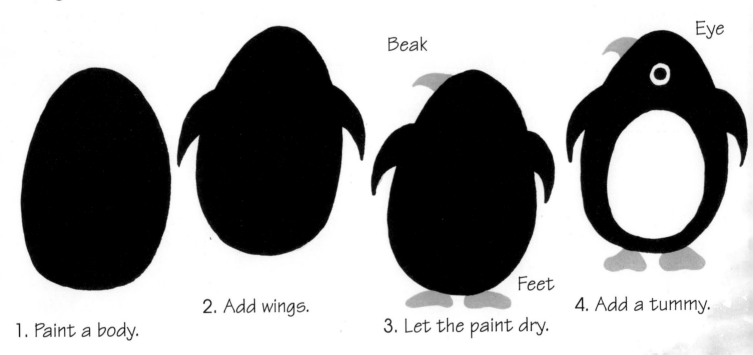

Beak

Eye

1. Paint a body.

2. Add wings.

3. Let the paint dry.

Feet

4. Add a tummy.

Fish

1.

2.

3.

Now how about... ducks on a frozen pond?

Paint flowers

Poppies

1. Make some swirly petal shapes with a pale candle.

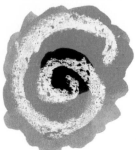

2. Paint over them like this.

Daisies

1. Draw loopy petal shapes with the candle.

2. Paint over them like this.

Tulips

1. Draw upright petal shapes with the candle.

2. Paint over them like this.

Buds

1. Draw small squiggles with the candle.

2. Paint over them like this.

Now how about... a big hat with flowers on it?

Paint a truck

1. Take an oblong sponge and dip the end in paint. Press it onto your paper.

2. Carefully print two more oblongs on either side of the first one.

3. For the engine, print a fourth oblong on its side in front of the first three.

Paint a busy road

Now try painting lots of trucks, vans and buses.

Use the big side of your sponge to print this van.

For the bus, use the long, narrow side of the sponge.

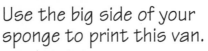

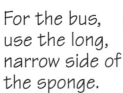

This small truck has three wheels.

You could add some road signs to your picture.

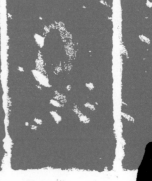

4. For the driver's cab, dip the end of a matchbox in paint and print two lines.

5. Use a round, cut potato to print wheels. Print a headlight using the end of a cork.

6. To make the road, dip crumpled paper in grey paint and press it along the paper under your truck.

It's fun to make up signs of your own.

Print windows with the end of a matchbox.

Use a matchbox to print the three oblongs on the front.

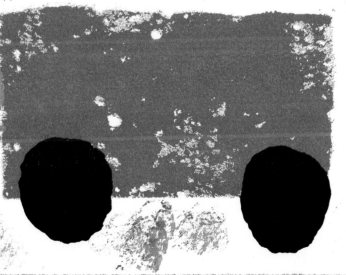

 Now how about... trucks driving onto a ferry boat?

Paint a bonfire

1. Take a piece of black paper and some runny yellow paint. Paint a bonfire shape.

2. Using runny red paint, add some wiggly stripes to your bonfire shape.

3. Using your fingers, mix the paint together to make flames.

6. Splash on some big sparks with your paintbrush. It's best to do this outside.

4. Crumple up some paper and dip it in white paint. Dab it on for the smoke.

5. Paint black sticks and logs. Don't worry if the paints mix.

Now how about... a firework display?

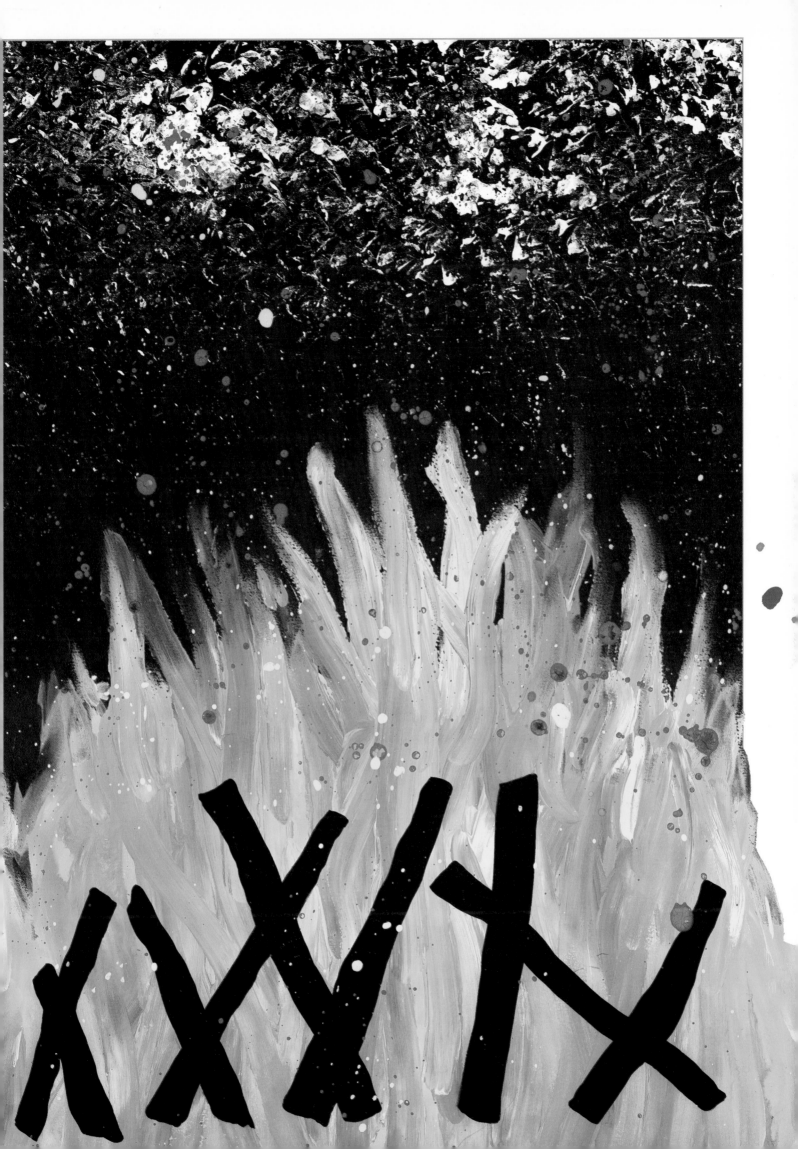

Paint a cactus in the desert

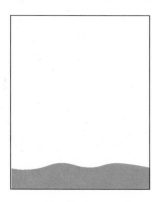

1. Paint a wiggly line for sand at the bottom of very large paper.

2. With a damp cloth, wipe on some paint for the sky.

3. In the same way wipe on some red streaks for clouds.

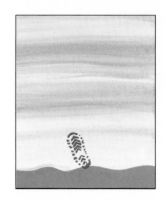

4. Paint the bottom of a clean rubber shoe or boot. Press it onto your paper.

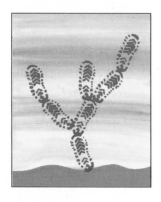

5. Make more overlapping shoe prints. Repaint the shoe each time.

6. Add pink flowers and a bright sun with a paintbrush.

7. Dip your fingers in orange paint and print some stones.

Cactus

Birds

Flowers

In the desert, some cacti grow taller than people.

Stones

Paint a sky picture

1. Cut cloud shapes
out of scrap paper.
Lay them on a large
sheet of thick paper.

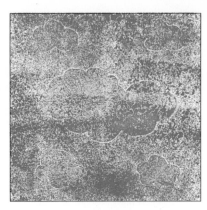

2. With a damp sponge,
gently dab blue paint
around the edges of all
your clouds.

3. When the whole
sheet of paper is
covered with blue, peel
the clouds off gently.

4. Paint some hot air
balloons in the sky.
Add some planes
doing exciting stunts.

5. When the planes
and balloons have
dried, decorate them
with bright patterns.

6. Add smoke trails to
the planes using a
piece of damp sponge
dipped in paint.

Now how about... kites in the sky?

Paint sheep in a field

1. Draw sheep's bodies and lambs' bodies on pieces of scrap paper. Cut them out.

2. Dip them in water. Shake off the drops, then arrange them on your painting paper.

3. Wind some yarn or wool around an old birthday card. You don't need to wind it very neatly. When the card is covered, tape down the end and cut off the leftover yarn.

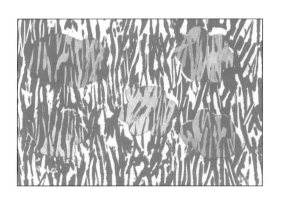

4. Paint the yarn green on one side. Press it all over your paper. Add more paint as you go.

5. Gently peel off the paper sheep. Paint on faces and legs with a fine paintbrush.

6. Add some flowers. Print them with a fingertip.

Now how about... rabbits on a hill?

Paint a face

1. Ask a grown-up to cut a big potato in half.

2. Dip the cut half of the potato in some paint. Print a face with it.

3. Mix some runny paint. Pour some along the top of your printed face.

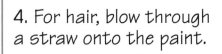

4. For hair, blow through a straw onto the paint.

5. Print the eyes with a finger dipped in paint.

Add long hair and a crown for a princess.

6. Paint the nose and the mouth.

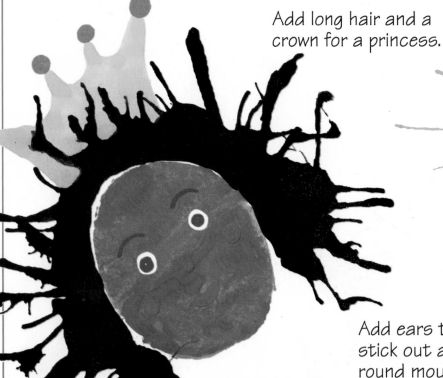

Add ears that stick out and a round mouth for a baby.

Now how about... some animals, using potato prints for the bodies?

For a clown, add bright hair, a red nose and a hat.

You could add a tangly beard as well as hair.

Try adding funny glasses or a bow tie.

57

Paint a scarecrow

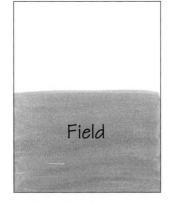

Field

Sky

Clouds

1. Dip a damp cloth in brown paint. Wipe it over about half your paper.

2. Still using a damp cloth wipe blue paint over the rest of your paper.

3. With a clean damp cloth blot some of the blue paint off again.

4. Thicken yellow paint with some flour. Finger-paint rows of corn.

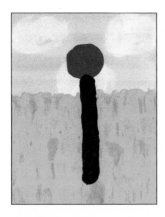

5. With thick paint, finger-paint a turnip-shaped head. Add a stick body.

6. Now finger-paint some clothes. Add eyes and a mouth and a carrot nose.

7. Dip the edge of some cardboard in yellow paint. Print some straw hair.

Paint pigs in some straw

Paint some pigs. You could use your fingers or a paintbrush.

Print the straw with the edge of some cardboard.

Now how about... some birds in a nest?

Paint fish in a waterfall

1. With a damp cloth, wipe blue stripes down your paper.

2. Add some green stripes to your paper in the same way.

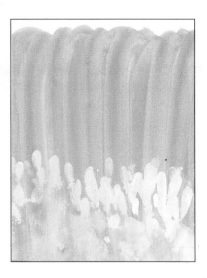

3. Make white handprints along the bottom of your paper.

4. Splash some white paint on with a brush to look like spray.

5. On another piece of paper paint lots of bright fish.

6. Let the paint dry. Add patterns on top.

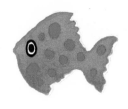

7. Cut the fish out. Glue them onto the waterfall picture.

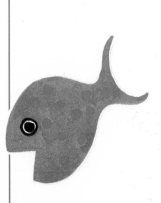

Now how about... an underwater picture with handprints for seaweed?

Paint a pattern

1. Mix flour with two
different shades of
paint to make it
really thick.

2. Cut an old
postcard in half.
Cut V shapes all
along one of the
shorter edges.

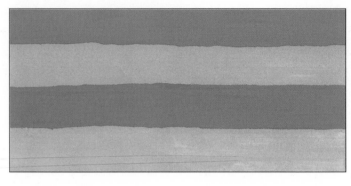

3. Take a big sheet of thick paper. Paint
some thick stripes on it using two shades.

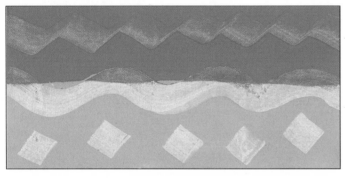

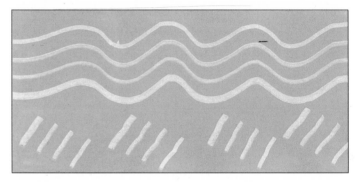

4. Scrape lots of different patterns into
the painted stripes using the straight
end of the card.

5. Then scrape patterns into the stripes
using the zigzag end of the card. Make
some straight and some wavy.

Butterfly

1. Paint thickly over a big sheet of paper.

2. Fold in half, painted side in.

3. Use a pencil to draw half a butterfly shape against the fold. Trace over the shape with your finger, pressing hard.

4. Open it out.

To change a pattern , paint over it and start again.

Paint more patterns

1. Fold a kitchen paper towel in half and in half again.

2. Fold it in half twice more, pressing hard.

3. Dip the corners into runny paint.

4. Put the folded paper towel between some sheets of newspaper. Roll over hard, with a rolling pin.

5. Take out the paper towel and open it very gently.

Other shapes

Fold a piece of paper towel into a triangle and dip the sides or the corners.

Fold a paper towel into a rectangle and dip each side of it in paint.

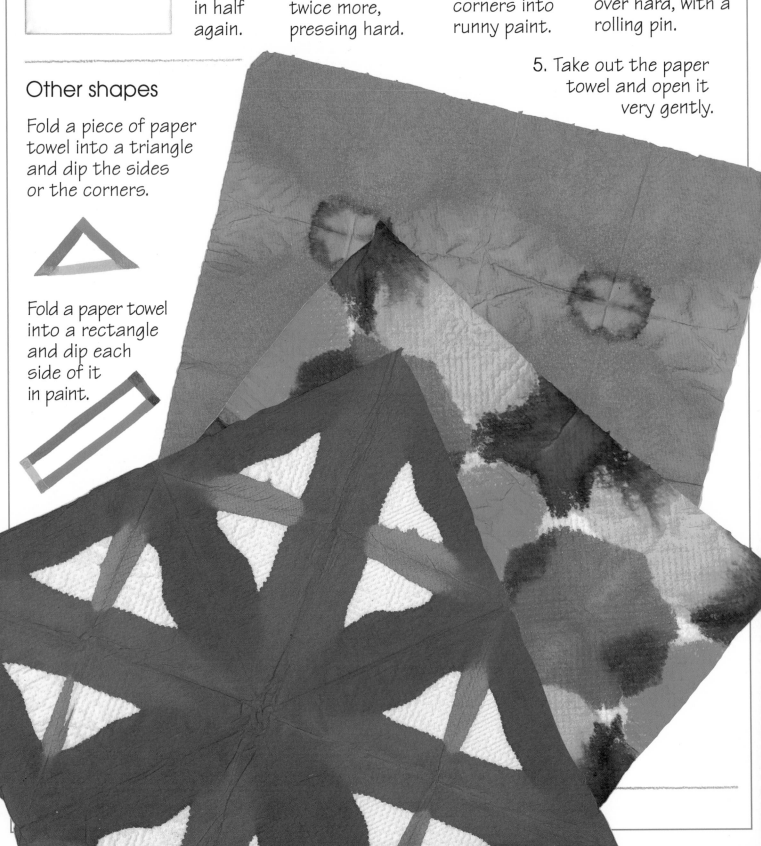

What shall I make?

Contents

Make a talking bird

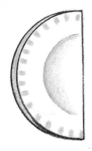    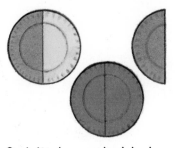 

You don't need these.

1. Fold three paper plates in half. Then, bend each one back along the fold.

2. Cut one plate along the fold. Cut a strip from the edge of one half.

3. Mix household glue (PVA) with red, orange and yellow paint. Paint the plates like this.

4. When the paint has dried, put the two whole plates together like this.

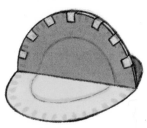 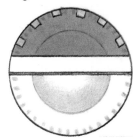

5. Tape or glue the orange and red parts together around the edge.

6. Turn it over and tape the orange piece onto the red half.

7. Make a roll of crêpe paper. Cut lots of slits in it.

8. Tape the paper onto the back of the yellow part.

9. Glue on paper eyes. You could glue on buttons for the middles.

You could add bright feathers instead of paper to the bird's head.

10. Cut a hole in a sock for your thumb and put your hand inside.

11. Put your hand into the bird. Open and close your hand to make it talk.

Make a wobbling head

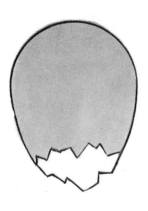   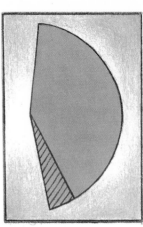

1. Paint a clean eggshell. Dry it upside down. Roll a ball of model dough the size of a marble.

2. Wet a finger and rub it on one side of the dough. Press it into the bottom of the egg.

3. Cut lots of pieces of yarn for hair. Glue them around the top of the eggshell.

4. Put tracing paper over the pattern for the hat on page 96. Draw over the lines carefully.

Sprinkle glitter onto dots of glue.

Add a pair of glasses and a gift wrap hat.

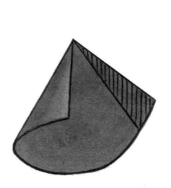

5. Glue the tracing paper onto bright paper with a glue stick. Cut around the shape.

6. Put glue on the shaded part of the pattern. Overlap the sides. Press them together.

7. Glue around the inside edge of the hat. Push the hat over the hair onto the head.

8. Paint a nose and a smiling mouth. Add middles to the eyes in a different shade.

Add lots of shapes all over the hat.

Cut a crown from shiny paper.

Make a parachute

1. Cut one side from a plastic carrier bag. Lay it flat.

2. Lay this book on top. Draw around it with a pen.

3. Cut it out. Fold over the top corner like this. Draw a line.

4. Fold the corner back up and cut along the line.

5. Poke a hole in each corner with a ballpoint pen.

6. Cut four pieces of thread as long as this book.

7. Poke one piece through one of the holes. Tie a knot.

8. Do the same with the other three corners.

9. Bring all the ends together. Tie them in a big knot.

10. Tape the knot to the back of a small model.

Fly your
parachute
outside. Crumple
it in your hand.
Put the model on
top and throw them
high into the air.

71

Make a furry snake

1. For the head, bend over one end of a pipecleaner.

2. Put it along a pencil and bend the head over the end.

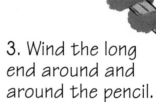

3. Wind the long end around and around the pencil.

4. Gently pull the snake halfway off the pencil.

5. Cut some paper eyes and glue them onto the head.

6. Draw a red tongue. Cut it out and glue it on.

72

Make some bangles

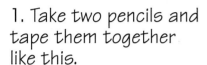

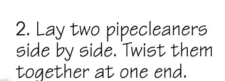

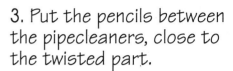

1. Take two pencils and tape them together like this.

2. Lay two pipecleaners side by side. Twist them together at one end.

3. Put the pencils between the pipecleaners, close to the twisted part.

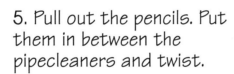

4. Twist the pipecleaners tightly next to the pencils, three times.

5. Pull out the pencils. Put them in between the pipecleaners and twist.

6. Keep on doing this to the end. Press the twisted pipecleaners flat.

7. Bend them into a circle. Twist the ends together.

Make a mask

  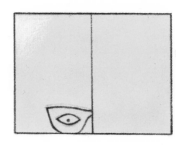 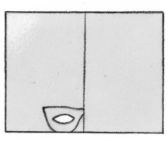

1. Take some stiff paper as big as this book. Fold it in half, short sides together.

2. Put some sunglasses along the bottom, halfway across the fold.

3. Draw around the shape. Add an eye, then poke a hole in it with a pencil.

4. Push scissors into the hole. Cut to the edge of the eye, then cut it out.

Glue on shiny shapes and sequins.

5. Fold the paper again. Draw around the eye shape onto the paper below.

6. Cut out the other eye shape. Fold the paper and draw a spiky shape.

7. Cut out the shape through both layers. Cut off the bottom corner.

8. Turn the mask over and paint it. Glue on lots of paper shapes.

9. Poke holes in the sides with a pencil. Tie on elastic to fit round your head.

Rip thin strips of tissue paper for a cat mask.

Make some vegetable people

1. Wash and dry a large potato. Cut a slice off one end so that it stands up.

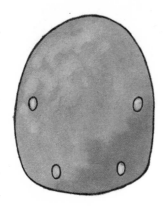

2. Poke four holes in the front of the potato with a sharp pencil.

3. Cut two pipecleaners in half. Push a piece into each hole.

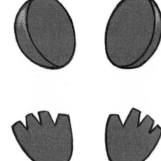

4. Make hands and feet from small balls of model dough.

5. Press the hands and feet onto the ends of the pipecleaners.

6. Make a face by adding a round nose and a smiling mouth.

7. Press on two circles for eyes. Add smaller middles to them.

8. Press dough through a sieve and scrape it off with a knife. Press it on.

A flower hat

Ball of model dough

 Strip of dough

Flat dough

Push the ball onto the flat piece. Roll up lots of strips to make flowers. Press them on.

A tall hat

Roll of dough

Circle of dough

Add a band.

A bag

 Squashed ball of dough

Add a handle.

Add a clip.

You can make people from all types of vegetables.

77

77

What shall I make today?

Make bread shapes

These bread shapes are decorations only. Do not eat them.

1. Press a big cookie cutter firmly into a slice of white bread.

2. Push the shape gently out of the cutter.

3. Make a hole by pressing the end of a straw into the shape.

4. Put it onto a baking rack and leave it overnight to go hard.

5. Mix a little paint with household glue (PVA). Paint the edges of the shape.

6. Paint the top. When it is dry, turn it over and paint the other side.

78

7. Glue on lots of glitter, sequins or beads to decorate your shape.

8. Push thread through the hole. Bring the ends together to make a loop.

9. Push the ends of the thread through the loop to make a knot.

Make paper flowers

A daisy

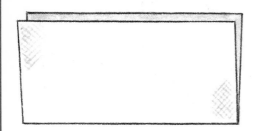

1. Fold a sheet of kitchen paper towel in half. Open it out. Cut along the fold.

2. Fold one piece in half, long sides together. You don't need the other piece.

3. Draw lots of stripes along the paper with a felt-tip pen.

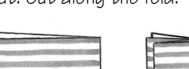 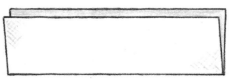

4. Fold in half with the short sides together, then fold it in half again.

5. Make long cuts close together from the bottom. Don't cut all the way up.

6. Open it carefully, so that it looks like this.

7. Tape one end of the paper onto a bendable straw. Roll the paper tightly around it.

8. Fasten the loose end with tape. Pull all the petals down.

9. Snip little pieces of yellow paper or yarn. Glue them into the middle.

You can use tissue paper for bright flowers. Cut the paper the same size as a piece of paper towel.

Another flower

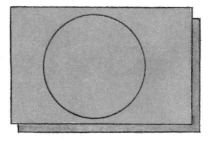

1. Take two sheets of tissue paper. Put a small plate or saucer on top and draw around it.

2. Cut around the circle through both layers of tissue paper. Fold them in half and in half again.

3. Twist the corner and tape onto the end of a straw. Gently pull the petals apart.

4. Make a ball of tissue paper and glue it in the middle.

Make a fish

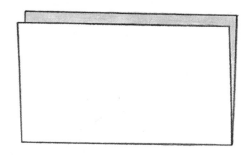

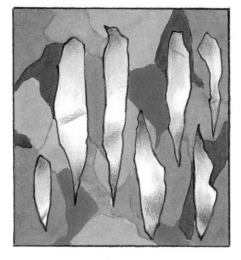

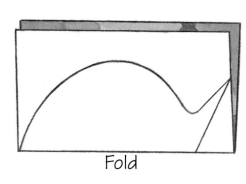

Fold

1. Fold a piece of paper in half, long sides together. Open it. Crease it back along the same fold.

2. Open the paper. Tear pieces of tissue paper. Glue them on. Add lots of strips of kitchen foil.

3. Fold the paper in half. Crease the fold well. Draw half a fat fish shape. Cut it out.

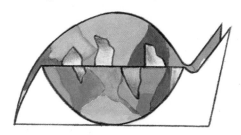

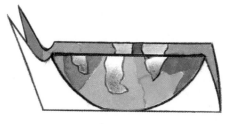

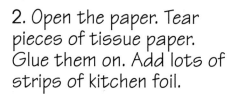

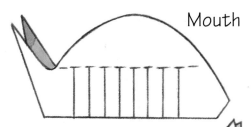

Mouth

4. Bend over one of the top edges until it touches the fold at the bottom. Press hard to crease it.

5. Turn the fish over. Bend the other top edge over in the same way. Remember to crease it well.

6. Unfold the top pieces. Snip a mouth. Make cuts as wide as your finger, up to the fold.

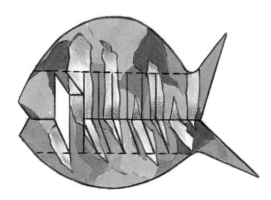

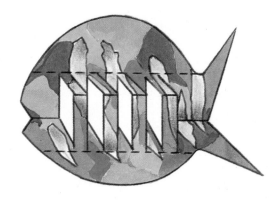

7. Half open the fish. Hold the head and pull the first strip out. Pinch the fold in the middle so that it stands up.

8. Skip the next strip. Pull out the next one. Go on in the same way until you reach the last strip. Pinch all the folds well.

Use bright
thread to
hang up
your fish.

Make model dough babies

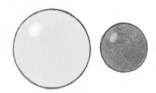

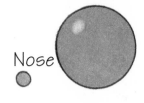

1. Make a ball of pink and yellow model dough, the sizes above. Roll them together.

2. Break off a tiny piece and roll the rest back into a ball. Press on the nose.

3. Press in eyes with a pencil. Press a mouth with the end of a straw.

4. Make a ball this size. Use a round pencil like a rolling pin to make it flat.

5. Turn a mug upside down and press it on. Peel away the spare dough.

6. Press a pencil point around the edge to make it lacy. Turn it over.

7. Put the head near the top. Press on a sausage shape for the body.

8. Wrap one side around the body, then wrap the other side over the top.

9. Gently press the blanket around the baby's head and neck.

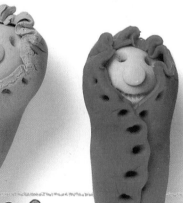

Make an octopus

1. Roll a model dough sausage. Flatten it. Roll balls for eyes and press them on.

2. Push a pencil point into each eye. Make a mouth with the end of a spoon.

3. Use scissors to snip eight tentacles. Bend up the side ones.

4. Press the end of a straw into the legs, to make lots of suckers.

5. Make seaweed from strips of green dough. Cut out some fish.

Make a row of clowns

1. Put tracing paper over the clown pattern on page 96. Draw over the black lines.

2. Draw around all the red lines with a red pencil. Take the paper off.

3. Carefully cut around the black lines, but don't cut out the clown.

 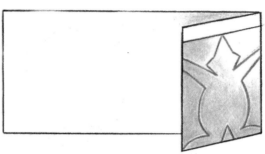

4. Glue the tracing onto the corner of a long sheet of stiff paper.

5. Turn the paper over. Fold the clown to the front. Crease along edge.

6. Turn the paper over again. Neatly fold the clown back to the front.

7. Turn it over. Fold it to the front again. Cut off the extra paper at the top and side.

8. Cut out the clown along the red lines. Don't cut the black lines at the edges.

9. Pull the clowns open, so that the tracing is on the back. Draw their hats.

10. Draw the clowns' faces. Use paint or felt-tip pens to decorate their clothes.

Make a crown

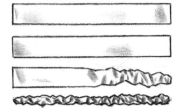

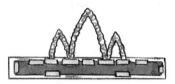
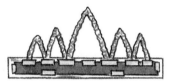

1. Cut a band of stiff paper to fit around your head, plus a little bit.

2. Lay it on a bigger piece of kitchen foil. Fold the edges in and tape them down.

3. Cut four strips of foil as wide as the band. Squeeze them to make thin sticks.

4. Bend one in half. Tape it onto the middle of the band, at the back.

5. Cut a little from the end of two pieces. Bend them and tape them on.

6. Cut the last piece in half. Bend each piece. Tape them on at each end.

7. Cut shiny shapes. Tape them on so you can see them above the band.

For an icy crown, use only blue and silver paper.

8. Turn the band over. Glue on scraps of bright paper or foil.

Make a smaller crown for a ballerina.

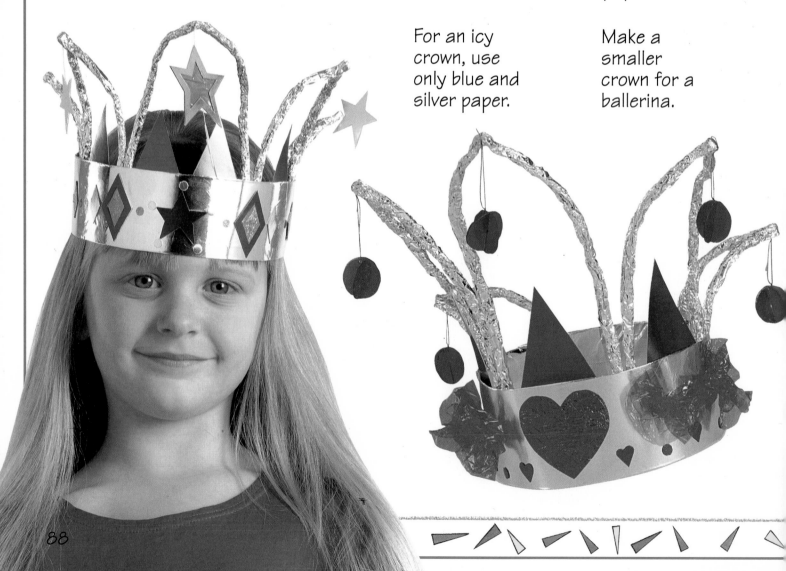

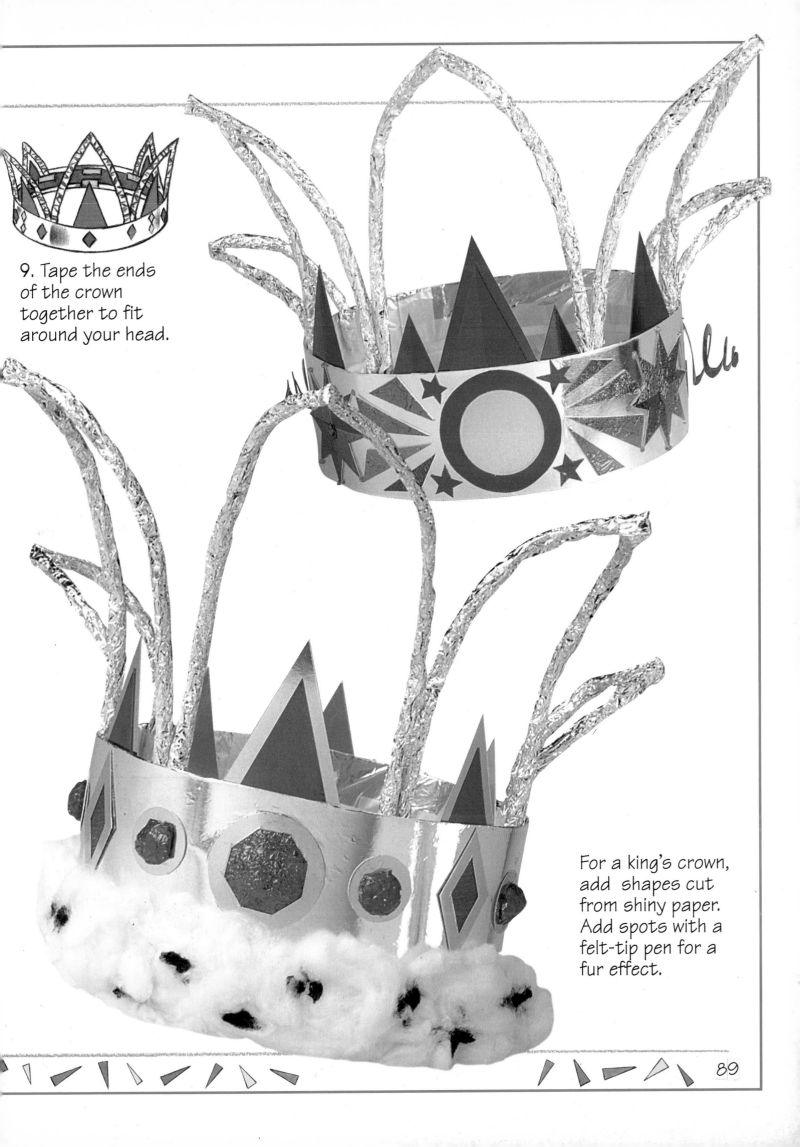

9. Tape the ends of the crown together to fit around your head.

For a king's crown, add shapes cut from shiny paper. Add spots with a felt-tip pen for a fur effect.

Make a lacy card

1. Draw some leaves, flowers and hearts on thick white paper.

2. Wrap sticky tape around the end of a darning needle to make a handle. Lay several kitchen paper towels over a folded newspaper. Put your drawing on top.

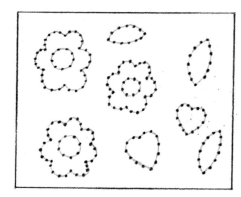

3. Use the needle to prick around the shapes. Press quite hard.

4. Cut around all the shapes very carefully. Leave a narrow edge around the holes.

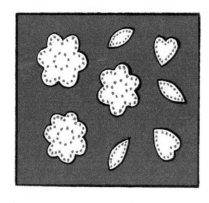

5. Dab glue stick on the pencil side of each shape. Press them very gently onto thin cardboard.

6. To make a card, glue your picture onto a slightly bigger piece of folded cardboard.

Make stamps

Draw a stamp and prick around the edges. Tear it carefully along the holes.

You don't need to use
white paper for all
your shapes.

Prick a wavy line
around your shape
Cut around it, but
leave a narrow edge.

Make a caterpillar

1. Put this book onto a piece of bright paper. Draw around it and cut it out.

You don't need this piece.

2. Fold it in half. Cut along the fold. Sponge different paint on both sides of one piece.

3. Fold the paper in half and in half again. Open it and cut along all the folds.

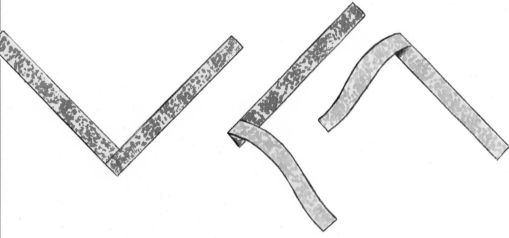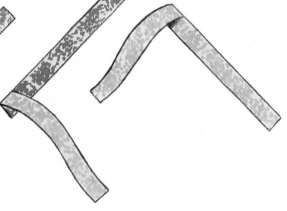

4. Put some glue at the end of one strip and join it to another one like this.

5. Fold the left strip over and crease it. Fold the other strip down over it.

6. Keep folding one strip over the other one to make a concertina shape.

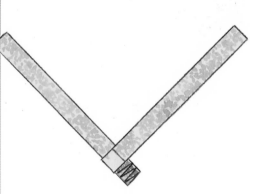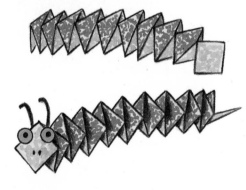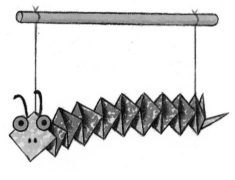

7. When you get near to the end of the strips, glue on the spare strips, then keep on folding.

8. When you reach the end glue down the top piece. Trim the ends. Add eyes, feelers and a tail.

9. Tape some thin elastic behind the head and the tail. Tie the caterpillar onto a straw.

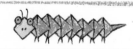

Make a brooch

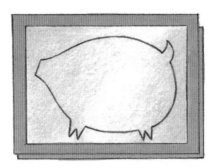

1. Put tracing paper over the pig pattern on page 96. Draw around the shape.

2. Put two pieces of felt together. Pin the tracing paper pattern on top.

3. Cut around the shape. Ask for help for the tricky parts. Take out the pins.

4. Cut the tail from one pig. Trace the pig's ear on page 96. Cut one out from felt.

5. Pin the pigs together. Sew around them with big stitches. Take out the pins.

6. Now sew close to the edge with tiny stitches. Leave a gap at the bottom.

Draw stripes on with a pen.

Glue sequins and beads onto your brooch.

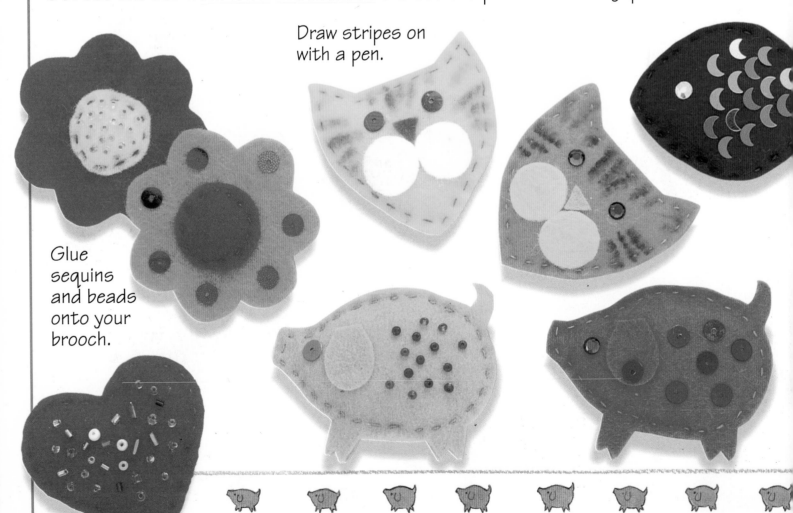

7. Take out the big stitches. Carefully push some stuffing into the hole.

8. Sew up the hole. Glue on the ear. Draw an eye with a felt-tip pen.

9. Turn the pig over. Sew a safety pin onto the back of the brooch.

The patterns for the other brooches shown here are on page 96.

Patterns

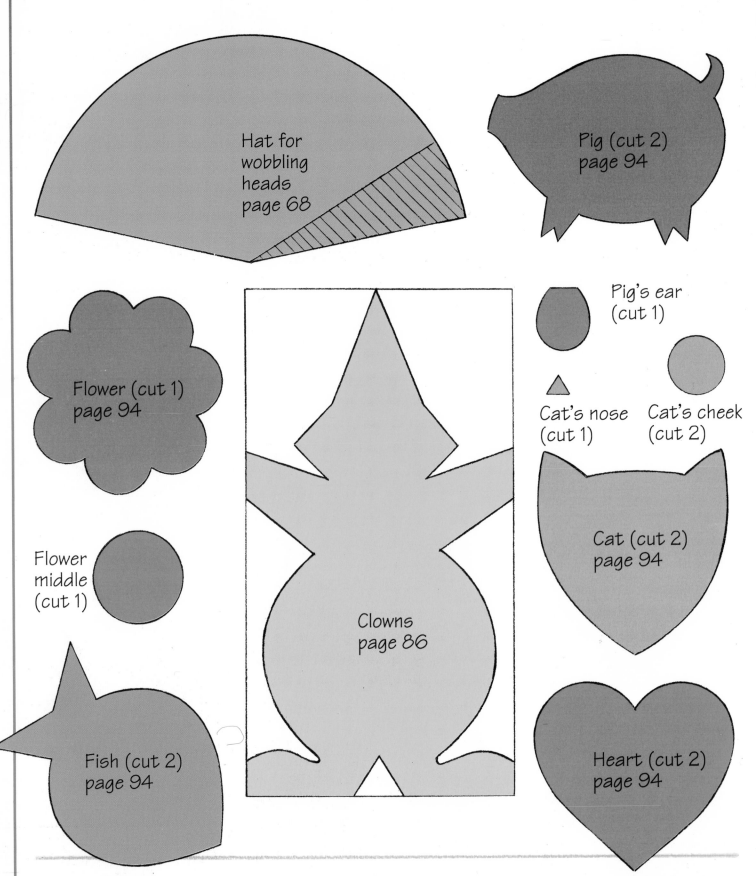

Hat for
wobbling
heads
page 68

Pig (cut 2)
page 94

Flower (cut 1)
page 94

Pig's ear
(cut 1)

Cat's nose
(cut 1)

Cat's cheek
(cut 2)

Flower
middle
(cut 1)

Clowns
page 86

Cat (cut 2)
page 94

Fish (cut 2)
page 94

Heart (cut 2)
page 94